iUniverse books may be ordered through booksellers or by contacting:

iUniverse
1663 Liberty Drive
Bloomington, IN 47403
www.iuniverse.com
1-800-Authors (1-800-288-4677)

ISBN: 978-1-5320-8567-3 (sc)
ISBN: 978-1-5320-8568-0 (e)

Library of Congress Control Number: 2019916238

Print information available on the last page.

iUniverse rev. date: 10/14/2019

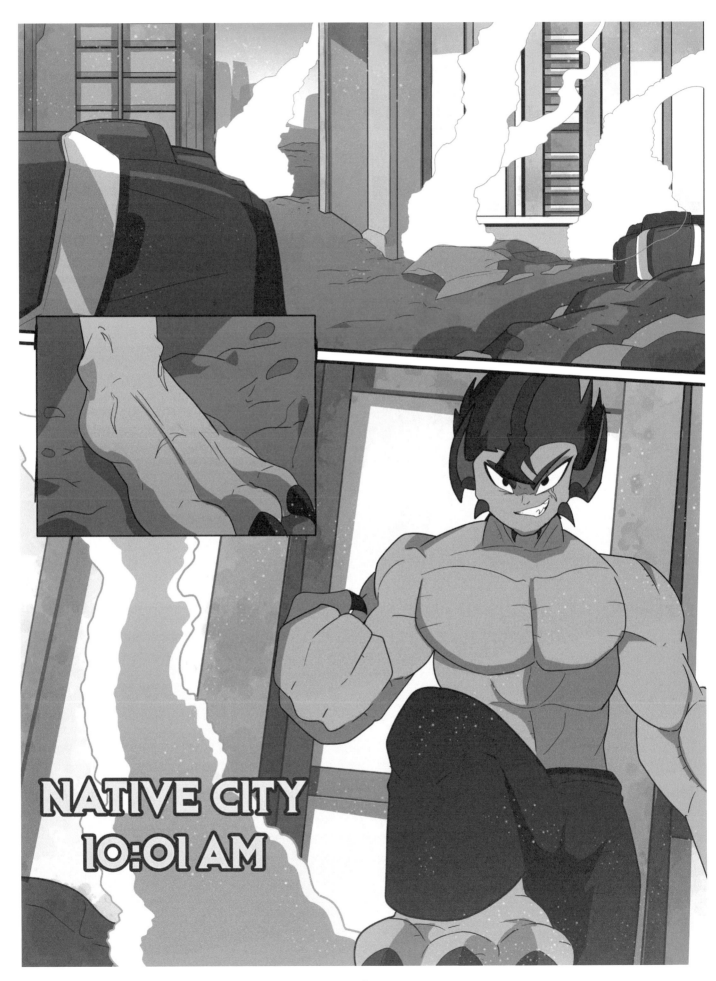

NATIVE CITY
10:01 AM

3

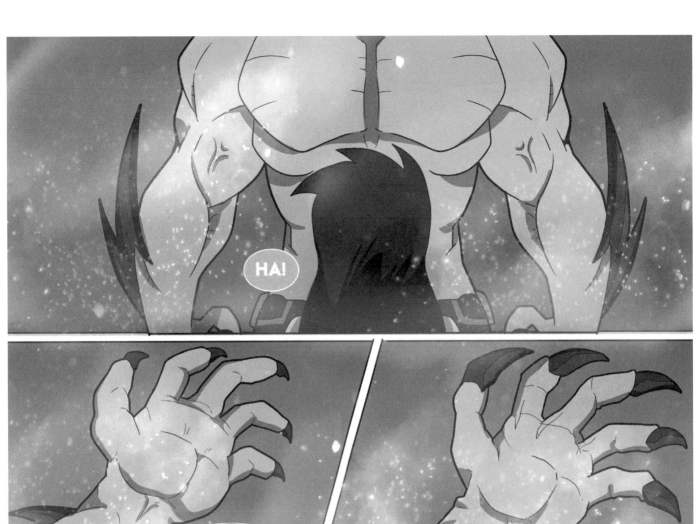

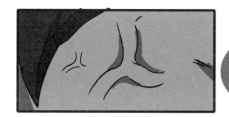

7

THAT'S MY OLDER SISTER, GWEN NATRES, SHE'S AN EVOLVED XZAPIAN.

A HUMAN BORN WITH NATURAL GENETICS MODIFICATION OR EVO POWER.

ALLOWING HER TO HAVE INCREDIBLE ABILITIES BASED ON HOW MUCH SHE CAN CONTROL HER EVO POWER.

SHE RUNS AN ORGANIZATION ALONGSIDE HER PARTNERS TO TRAIN YOUNG KIDS STRUGGLING TO CONTROL THEIR EVO POWER.

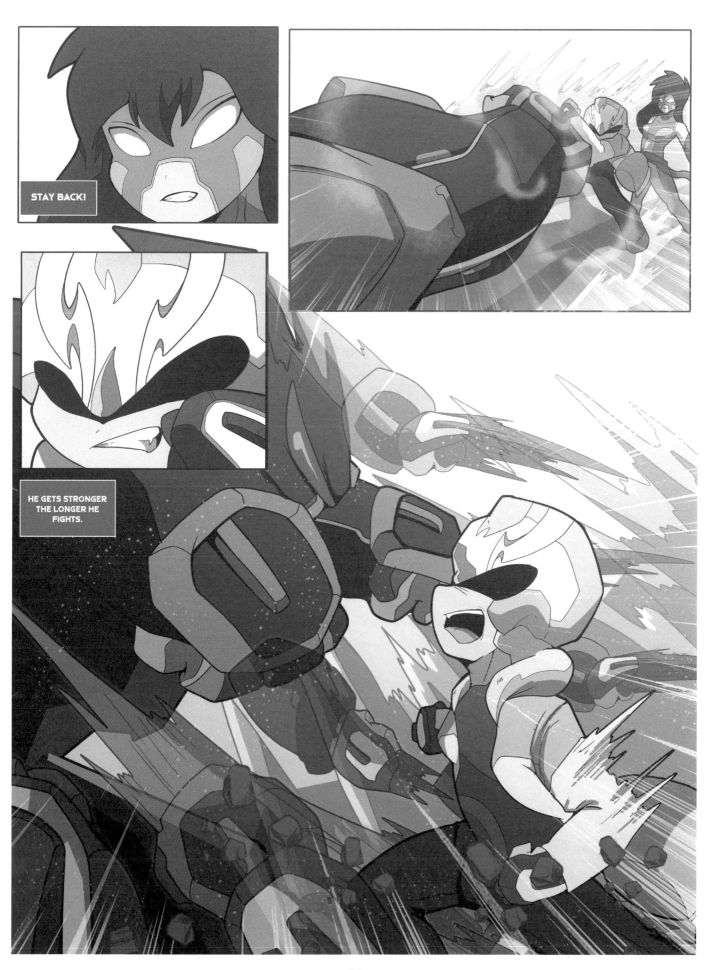

STAY BACK!

HE GETS STRONGER
THE LONGER HE
FIGHTS.

ILLUSION
TAKEDOWN!

11:05 AM

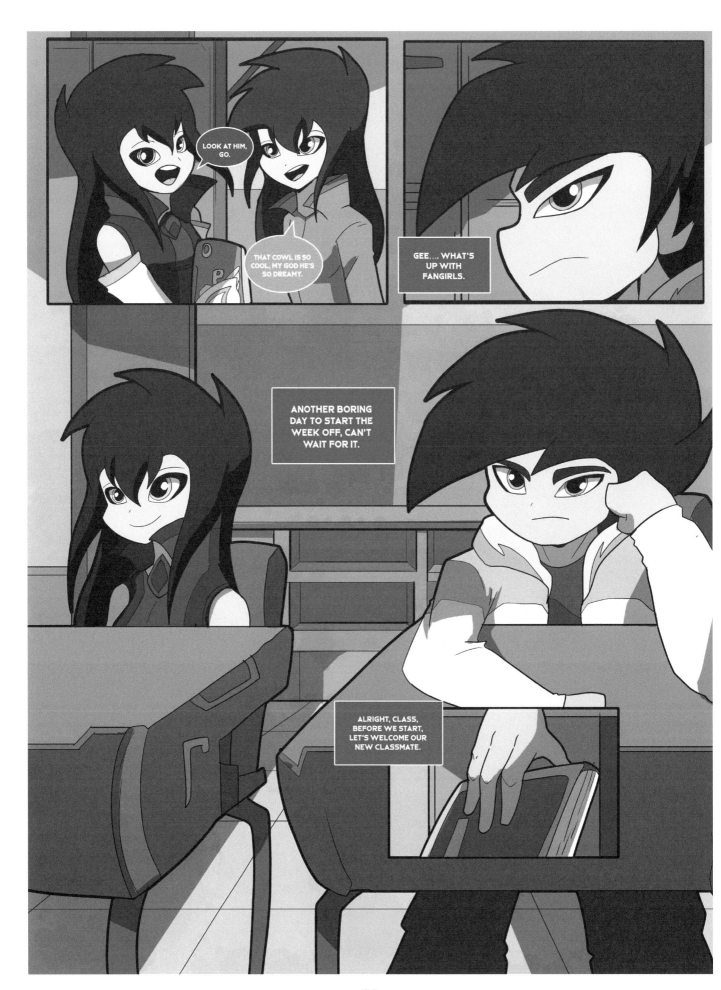

CLASSMATE?

MY NAME IS KORI TADASHI.

HOPE THAT WE GET ALONG.

JIN-9

THE END

21

Printed in the United States
By Bookmasters